MEET THE New Kids ON THE BLOCK

D1571078

Contributing Author: Jae-Ha Kim

Photo Credits:
Stephen P. Allen/Gamma-Liaison: 36, 58, 89, 92; Julian
Barton/London Features International: 80, 106, 109; Larry
Busacca/Retna Ltd.: 9, 19, 21, 24, 27, 34, 39, 44, 45, 48, 49,
55, 67, 69, 71, 75 (bottom), 76, 79, 84, 87, 88, 94, 104,
118, 121; R.J. Capak/London Features International: 119;
Gary Czvekus/Retna Ltd.: 100; Greg De Guire/Celebrity Photo:
57, 81; Scott Downie/Celebrity Photo: 97; Felix/Star File: 65;
Janet Gough/Celebrity Photo: 33, 73; Steve Granitz/Retna: 38,
42, 63, 74, 111, 117; Caroline Greyshock/Columbia Records:
28; Todd Kaplan/Star File: 7, 113, 115, 125; Jeff
Katz/Columbia Records: 107; Dave Lewis/London Features
International: 35; Victor Malafronte/Celebrity Photo: 15; J.
Mayer/Star File: 91, 123; John Paschal/Celebrity Photo: 23, 30,
37, 43, 46, 54, 101; Robin Platzer/Images: 16; Ebet Roberts:
53, 64, 75 (top), 127; Jennifer Rose: 90; Steve
Schapiro/Gamma-Liaison: Front Cover; David Seelig/Star File:
13, 85, 105; Jeff Slocomb/Outline Press: 47, 77; J.
Smith/London Features International: 82, 120; Barry
Talesnick/Retna Ltd.: 60; Scott Weiner/Retna Ltd.: 127
(bottom); Ron Wolfson/London Features International: 98;
Vinnie Zuffante/Star File: 12, 52, 56, 62, 66, 68, 70, 93, 102.

Color Section:
Larry Busacca/Retna, Ltd; Steve Granitz/Retna Ltd.; Todd
Kaplan/Star File; Dave Lewis/London Features International;
Eddie Malluk/Retna Ltd.; Elizabeth Marshall/Picture Group; Paul
Natkin/Photo Reserve; Ebet Roberts; Steve Schapiro/Gamma-
Liaison; Jeff Slocomb/Outline Press; J. Smith/London Features
International.

CONTENTS

MAKE ROOM FOR THE NEW KIDS

There's no contest when it comes to naming the cutest group in rock 'n' roll today. New Kids on the Block wins hands down.

But the five guys from Boston are proving that they're more than just pretty faces. The New Kids on the Block are making musical history, and they have you to thank for it. When older people laughed at the New Kids, calling them "manufactured" and "teeny-bop idols," you held their pictures close to your hearts and their music close to your ears.

"Our fans always knew more about good music than a lot of the critics who were trashing our records," says New Kid Donnie Wahlberg. "They're the ones responsible for all the success we've achieved over the past couple years.

"We're about as manufactured as any other band on the charts today. To a certain extent, any group that has a

The New Kids are *(standing, left to right)* **Jordan Knight, Danny Wood, Jon Knight,** *(kneeling, left to right)* **Donnie Wahlberg, and Joe McIntyre.**

record contract is 'manufactured' by how its record company wants to present them. The fact that we're all young adds fuel to the fire. It's easier to say *we're* manipulated by adults than accusing a group that's band members are, say, 25 or 30, of the same thing. People are more likely to believe that younger people are more naive."

Today, the New Kids are leaping up the charts and laughing all the way to the bank. The group has gone from opening act to headliner in less than two years. Major magazines have written stories about the boys, and television news programs have aired clips of screaming concertgoers who can't get enough of them.

It's difficult now to believe that the group's record company really wasn't sure how people would react when it signed the New Kids to a recording contract in 1986. But, the boys *were* young and unseasoned, and Columbia Records questioned whether there was a market for the New Kids on Top 40 radio.

The New Kids answered Columbia's questions with one hit single after another, including the Top Ten tunes "Please Don't Go Girl," "You Got It (The

The boys in the band are enjoying their success, but they insist they're still a bunch of average guys.

Right Stuff)," "I'll Be Loving You (Forever)," and "Hangin' Tough," all from their explosive second album, *Hangin' Tough.*

In addition, the New Kids have a list of accomplishments that even their older peers would envy. Besides being the first teen group to have a number-one single and a number-one album at the same time, the New Kids are also the first act since 1980 to have three singles in the Top 40 at the same time. What's more, their album *Hangin' Tough* has sold more than seven million copies.

So if there wasn't a market for them back in 1986, there certainly is now. The New Kids have carved out their own place on the charts with their funky music and cool videos. (Who can forget their fab video for "Cover Girl," in which a lucky young lady gets to dance with Donnie?) The kids also receive 30,000 fan letters every month.

The guys are not about to forget their fans, either. That's why they work so hard to make sure you'll have plenty of New Kids material to see and hear. The New Kids' new album, *Step By Step,* is a giant step in that direction. It's a winning blend of rap, rock, and funk. So if you haven't gotten hold of a copy yet, better start saving your allowance. After all, the album's for you.

The New Kids are also hoping that this album will prove to critics that they are more than just another cute band. The New Kids point out that if they were just cute, fans wouldn't stand in line for hours to buy tickets to their concerts. And it's undeniable that they are a hot draw.

Fortunately for the New Kids, teen singer Tiffany was quick to pick up on the boys' potential. When she went on her first major tour in 1988, she picked the New Kids to be her opening act. The tables were turned in 1989, when the New Kids became headliners themselves. They returned the favor by asking her to be their opening act when they toured during the summer of that year.

Though various members of the band have been rumored to be romantically interested in the red-haired singer, Donnie denies this.

"She's like a sister to us," he insists. "We all think she's really pretty and talented, and we love her like she's a member of our family. I think she feels that way about us, too."

continued on page 14

The boys were all smiles as they helped their pal Tiffany celebrate her 18th birthday.

Jonathan, Joe, Donnie, and Danny demonstrate some rad dance moves for their fans.

She certainly does. When asked about what it was like to tour with the New Kids, she says, "I adore them, too! They are just the nicest guys. We're all about the same age, so we'd have fun just talking about kid things. I know a lot of girls would love to have been in my shoes."

Unfortunately, most fans aren't as lucky as Tiffany. For those of you who can't be in Tiffany's shoes, Hasbro Toys has the next best thing—New Kids dolls. The dolls, which stand about a foot tall, would make even Barbie and Ken jealous.

When the dolls go on the market (Hasbro says it's likely to be in the Fall of 1990), you'll be able to choose between two versions of each guy. One will be dressed in casual streetwear. The other will be wearing funky stage wear, just like the clothes the boys really wear in concert. Each doll will come with a replica of a microphone. A cassette tape of an exclusive New Kids interview will also be included.

Other things Hasbro has in store for New Kids fans include a New Kids concert-stage play set, with a special stand that allows each doll to dance to a

The boys held a press conference at the Hard Rock Cafe in New York City to introduce Hasbro's new line of New Kids dolls.

You'll have no trouble deciding which of the New Kids dolls is modelled after Joey Joe. Like the *real* doll, this little guy has beautiful blue eyes.

song; tiny guitars, amplifiers, microphones, and keyboards; a sleek telephone adorned with a New Kids logo; a real microphone that lets you tune into a radio station and sing along with the guys; and a portable cassette player with headphones. And for those of you who have never been patient enough to piece together a jigsaw puzzle, we bet you'll be anxious to get your hands on Hasbro's poster-size puzzles with pictures of the New Kids on them.

Why did Hasbro, the world's largest toy maker, choose the New Kids on the Block over other popular acts, such as Madonna, Tiffany, and Def Leppard? Just what is it about the New Kids that makes them so unique? After all, they're certainly not the first teen idols, nor will they be the last. Your older sisters may remember performers such as David Cassidy, his brother Shaun, the Bay City Rollers, and Andy Gibb. They all leapt up the record charts, but none of them had the phenomenal success the New Kids on the Block are enjoying.

"The New Kids have struck a chord with kids everywhere," enthuses Al Carosi, a senior vice president of marketing at Hasbro. "We're excited to be working with a group of young men who have brought so much enjoyment to so many people."

Donnie puts it more simply. "I think one reason people like us is because we're just us. We're real average."

They may think that they're just an average group of guys, but fans across the country—and around the world—know better. They know that the New Kids on the Block are truly something special.

What will happen to the New Kids when they grow from boys into men? Will the fans still be loyal to them? The guys think so (and so do we), but it's not something they're worrying about. They all intend to remain in the music business in one form or another.

Donnie already has taken a step towards getting into the production end of the business. On the New Kids' seasonal album, *Merry, Merry Christmas,* he cowrote "Funky, Funky Xmas."

"I had a blast working on that song," Donnie says. "It felt great to be able to stretch as an artist. Writing is something that I'm definitely interested in, and am eager to do more of."

The boys may soon be getting into

more than music, though. Several film companies, including Disney and 20th Century Fox, are courting the boys to make their acting debuts. And the three major television networks are interested in getting a New Kids cartoon series going. So far, no deals have been finalized. But that's not worrying the New Kids either.

"We intend on being around forever. So get prepared for that now!" says Donnie.

To paraphrase an old saying, rock 'n' roll is here to stay...and so are the New Kids on the Block.

The New Kids are reaching for the stars!

BUILDING THE NEW KIDS, BLOCK BY BLOCK

It's undeniable that the New Kids on the Block are one of today's hottest *and* coolest bands. Even many of the hipsters who read *Rolling Stone* magazine picked the New Kids, along with Living Colour, Indigo Girls, Skid Row, and Warrant, as "Best New American Band" in the magazine's 1989 readers poll.

But what do you know about how the band was formed? Did the New Kids all know each other when they were younger? Did they meet at an audition?

In a way, the New Kids on the Block is a "manufactured" band, as were the Monkees in the 1960's, Menudo in the 1970's, and New Edition in the early 1980's. Some people have criticized the band for this, but you know that doesn't make a difference. After all, the only thing that matters is how they sound. And anyone who has heard them sing can vouch for the fact that they sound great!

When record producer Maurice Starr decided that he wanted to form a new band, he began searching for talented boys in the Boston area. He and his assistants spent six months in 1984 auditioning about five hundred teenagers who wanted to be in the band.

Out of all those who tried out, Donnie was the first to be selected. Besides the fact that he was handsome, outspoken, intelligent, talented, and very mature for a 15-year-old, Donnie also had something that can't be taught in

Donnie was the first New Kid to be selected, and he's been a driving force in the band ever since.

school. Donnie had charisma. When he sang, he commanded attention. Maurice knew this was an important factor for any successful entertainer. He knew Donnie had what it took to attract fans, and he was right.

Building the group around Donnie came about rather simply. Once Donnie was asked to be in the group, he began suggesting other boys he thought would be good for the group. The first person he suggested was his best friend, Danny Wood. Although Maurice was skeptical at first about Danny's talent, his doubts were put to rest after he heard Danny sing. The quiet, handsome Danny proved he was a power-house performer.

Once Donnie and Danny had secured their positions in the band, they convinced Maurice to listen to their friend Jordan sing. Although he was just 14, Jordan already had developed a singing style all his own. He could sing falsetto as well as rumble out a funky rap tune. And it didn't hurt that he had the awesome looks of a movie star.

Once Jordan was in, he knew that the perfect addition to the group would be his 16-year-old brother, Jonathan. The two boys had grown up singing together

They may argue every once in a while, but brothers Jordan and Jonathan Knight are thankful that they have each other around for support.

in their church choir, and they knew the importance of singing in harmony. So Jonathan auditioned and got an instant thumbs-up from Maurice and the other boys.

By 1985, New Kids on the Block was shaping up just fine. With four singers who could dance, they were assured of taking the music world by storm. But Maurice Starr was smart enough to know that the band could attract even more fans if it included a member who was just a little bit younger than the other boys. After all, the younger listeners needed a boy they could relate to, as well.

Joe began his performing career at the age of six.

Young Joe McIntyre turned out to be the perfect final addition to the New Kids on the Block. At 13 years of age, Joe was blessed with both an innocent peaches-and-cream face and a voice that wouldn't quit. As a former child actor, he was also used to performing in front of audiences. And, having grown up in a large family, he knew how to hold his own with the other boys in the band.

Donnie, Jonathan, Jordan, Danny, and Joe all admit they were nervous when they auditioned. After all, they were just Boston kids who enjoyed singing and playing basketball. Maurice Starr, on the other hand, was a famous multitalented musician who helped New Edition shoot to the top of the charts. Even though the boys were nervous about meeting Maurice, Starr says he knew the moment he met them that they were all potential stars.

By 1985, the boys in the band were performing together under the bizarre name Nynuk. With a name like that, it came as no surprise that the boys didn't achieve any success. After all, the name was more fitting for a beached whale than a heartthrob band. Even though the boys hated the name, Maurice insisted it was the perfect name for the group.

It was around that time that Maurice wrote a song for Nynuk called "New Kids on the Block." When the boys heard the song, they wanted to change their name to New Kids on the Block. Maurice insisted the change would be a mistake. He thought the name was too long and not catchy enough.

In a move that proved that the boys were eager to take some responsibility for their band, they insisted that the name be changed. Seeing how eager the kids were, Maurice gave in, and New Kids on the Block was officially christened.

With a fine new name, the boys were anxious to record and tour. But first, they had to drum up interest in the New Kids within the music industry. Unfortunately, they had two things going against them. They were young, and they were totally unknown. In the cut-throat music world, where millions of dollars are made and lost, few companies wanted to take a chance on a bunch of teenagers from Boston.

But the New Kids' impressive four-song demo tape finally landed in the right hands at Columbia Records. While Columbia was still a bit skeptical, it saw

The guys are always willing to take turns in the spotlight to please their fans. When this shot was taken, Jordan had center stage.

**One of the Kids' first big gigs
was a "Just Say No To Drugs"
concert.**

potential in the New Kids. So the label signed the band to a record deal in 1986. The New Kids' first single, "Be My Girl," became a hit on Boston radio stations, but few people outside of that city ever heard it.

The New Kids' debut album followed shortly afterwards. The guys spent much of 1986 and part of 1987 touring to promote their record. Although that album didn't go anywhere, people in the music industry began to notice the band. Word was out that the New Kids on the Block were on the move and that they were moving up.

The New Kids spent almost a full year recording *Hangin' Tough,* the album that would make them a household name across the country. The songs on that album were a far cry from the ones on *New Kids on the Block.* While the first album sounded sweet and pop, the new songs had a tough, street feel to them. The heavy dance beat made the songs catchy, but there was no doubt that the New Kids—and their music—had grown up.

It took the New Kids four years, but they became "overnight sensations." All you fans know what happened next. The

New Kids sold millions of records, they played to sell-out crowds at concerts around the country, and their normal lives became the focus of the press.

Although their popularity makes it difficult for the boys to keep up normal lives nowadays, they're willing to sacrifice their personal lives to make you happy. So, when you go to their concerts, show them your appreciation. Raise your hands high in the air and sing along. Send them letters and tell them how much you love them (you'll find their address on page 128). And keep on listening to their awesome music. That's the best way for you to let them know that they've got the right stuff.

The New Kids love performing for their fans.

MEET THE
NEW KIDS
ON THE BLOCK

It's hard to listen to the radio or watch videos on television without hearing the New Kids on the Block (and who's complaining?). But to be a true-blue New Kids fan, you have to know more than the names Donnie, Danny, Joe, Jordan, and Jonathan. You have to know where these guys are coming from and where they want to go. You have to know what they like and what they don't like. You have to know the name of Danny's pet fish, what kind of food Joe loves to munch on, and where you're likely to find Jordan when he's just hanging out. In other words, you have to meet the boys in the band.

DANNY WOOD

Born on May 14, 1969, Danny Wood has all the traits of a Taurus. He's as strong-willed as he is strong-minded. His good friend and bandmate Donnie Wahlberg describes Danny as "the best friend a guy could ever want to have," then quickly adds, "but just don't get him mad."

Danny is a little less flashy than some of the other boys when it comes to performing on stage. Although he's as good at the dance moves as Donnie and Jordan are, Danny says he likes doing things behind the scenes, so to speak, to make sure the concerts go just right.

His attention to exactness would have made him well-suited for his first professional ambition—to become an architect. Danny put that dream on hold, however, so that he could live out his fantasy of being a rock 'n' roll star.

Because he doesn't talk as much

continued on page 36

When Danny was young, he wanted to be an architect.

"Music has made a goal for us," says Danny.

Down-to-earth Danny still does his own laundry.

during interviews as some of the other New Kids do, Danny's fans have dubbed him shy. But Danny insists that he only seems shy to strangers. "Ask my brothers and sisters if they think I'm shy, and they'll tell you I'm not," he told *Teen Beat* magazine. The five-foot-eight, brown-eyed musician does admit, though, that while he's been on stage a lot, he still gets butterflies in his stomach before each night's performance.

A man of simple needs, Boston-born Danny says his life is quiet and laid back

Does this gorgeous guy look shy to you?

Danny tells his fans to hold on to their dreams and stay off the streets.

This muscle-bound boy loves to work out with weights.

when he's not on the road. He can get by just fine with a radio, his friend Calvin's cooking, and his pet fish, Mustard. He also enjoys playing keyboards, writing love songs, and playing sports, especially basketball.

Danny attributes his down-to-earth attitude to his upbringing. Danny's father, Daniel, Sr., is a mailman, and his mother, Elizabeth, is an administrative assistant, so

This romantic guy enjoys writing love songs.

Danny grew up knowing that money doesn't grow on trees. Even today, with all his wealth, Danny wisely invests his money rather than spending it on fad things.

What's this talented guy's advice to fans about how to become a star? "You have to start somewhere," he told *Teen Beat* magazine. "Don't be too proud, or all the opportunities will pass you by."

Although he's achieved more than he ever thought he would with the New Kids, Danny still has one dream that's unfulfilled. He wants to win a Grammy.

Hang tough, Danny. It shouldn't be much longer before that dream becomes reality.

DONNIE WAHLBERG

Often referred to as the smartest New Kid, Donnie is one of the group's strongest driving forces. When New Kids producer Maurice Starr was looking for a bunch of talented Boston boys to be in his new band, everyone he talked to told him to go see Donnie Wahlberg. Donnie, they said, was the kid who had the creative energy to take a group to the top.

Although Donnie was the first kid to join the band, his love of sports almost prevented him from going to the initial audition. "I was intimidated by Maurice's reputation at first," Donnie remembers. "I didn't want to go to the audition. I just wanted to play baseball."

After much thought, Donnie went to meet Maurice and was pleasantly surprised. Feeling at home with him, Donnie sang, rapped, and danced for

continued on page 44

"I like to be friendly and make people feel good."

Donnie pals around with a perky pooch backstage at the Nickelodeon Kids Choice Awards.

Maurice. Maurice, in turn, was impressed by Donnie's varied talents.

Donnie was no novice to rock 'n' roll when he met Maurice. At school dances and friends' parties, Donnie was the boy who could always be counted on to liven things up, whether it was with his right-on Michael Jackson imitations or his funky raps. At the tender age of 11, Donnie performed in a trio called Risk. He sang, played drums, and even did a song or two on the harmonica.

Donnie and Joe do a little jammin' during a break in rehearsal.

"I'm one of nine kids in our family," Donnie says. "So I guess my ham streak prevented me from getting lost in the shuffle. I liked getting attention from my parents."

Donnie was born on August 17, 1969, in Dorchester, a suburb of Boston. Being from the East helps him keep a level head on his shoulders, he says, because people back there aren't as star struck as those who live in California. A drummer at heart, Donnie insists that he'd be just as happy beating the skins as he is being at center stage.

Donnie shows off his awesome acrobatic skills during a New Kids concert. Be careful, Donnie!

Donnie is producing music for the Northside Boys.

Even though he's still a young man, Donnie is securing a future for himself in the music business. In addition to his work on and off stage for the New Kids, he's started writing songs for other groups. He's also been doing production work for an up-and-coming Boston rap group called The Northside Boys. And with fellow New Kids Danny and Jordan, Donnie is producing an album for singer Tommy Page.

"I think a good sign of potential longevity is being able to take care of yourself in business," says Donnie. "We plan on being around as a group for a

Donnie raps with Ronnie of the Northside Boys.

long time. But just to cover my own butt, I want to be on the production end of making records, too."

For those of you who dream of dating Donnie, there's both good news and bad news. The bad news is that he dates mostly older girls. A mature young man, Donnie breaks girls' hearts right and left (not on purpose, of course). It's his combination of charm and urban street

Donnie reaches out to his fans, who just can't resist his soulful singing.

smarts that just makes him irresistible. Although he's still young, Donnie admits he has a weakness for older women, like those in their late-20's. But the good news

Darling Donnie says he's always wanted to be famous. Well, Donnie, we're glad your wish has come true!

is that, so far, Donnie hasn't met a girl of any age that he hasn't liked.

"I like all kinds of girls," he says. "I haven't met one yet who hasn't had a special quality about her. I think they know I'm just a normal Joe, and so they relate to me. They don't think I'm some big super hero or anything."

Laughing, he adds, "That's a good thing, because I'm definitely not! I do normal things like go for drives and hang out at malls. My life really isn't that interesting."

As if to prove his point, he insists that a big day for him means shopping around for new clothes (sneakers are his obsession) or spending time with his bandmates and his family. Donnie describes himself as romantic, outgoing, and friendly. But Donnie's fans would probably want to add that he's also a major hunk.

"I look OK," he says, with his usual modesty. "I'm not as good-looking as Jordan!"

We don't know about that, Donnie. We'll have to call it a draw.

JORDAN KNIGHT

More than a few people have noticed the resemblance between Jordan Knight and actor Tom Cruise. But it's more than his dreamy good looks that have made Jordan so popular among New Kids fans in the United States.

This soulful singer has a romantic streak that girls just can't resist. Describing the New Kids song "I'll Be Loving You (Forever)," Jordan says it is a ballad that comes straight from the guys' hearts. The song is dedicated, he adds, to all the pretty girls in the world.

A definite ladies' man, Jordan finds all girls beautiful in one way or another, especially those who have an outgoing personality and great sense of humor. Jordan would like to find a girl who is very loving and who can express her emotions. Of course, he also enjoys spending time with girls who like to have fun.

This gorgeous guy always watches his manners when he's with a lady.

If you want to get Jordan's attention, just call him "J."

Do we have any young ladies out there who fit the bill? If so, there are some other things you might like to know about him.

Born on May 17, 1971, Jordan is a Taurus whose stubborn streak works to his advantage. He and the other guys stuck it out with New Kids on the Block even though the band's early days weren't exactly memorable. A dedicated worker, he gave up sleep, time with school friends, and a normal teenager's social life to help make New Kids a first-rate

continued on page 56

53

Jordan laughs off the jitters before a New Kids concert in Los Angeles.

Jordan used to be a soloist in his church
choir. Now he sings to faithful fans.

group. In other words, when he finds something he cares about, he's likely to stick with it through good times and bad.

Jordan likes to celebrate his birthday with his close friends and family. While his hectic schedule makes it difficult for him to relax as much as he'd like to, his birthday is the one day he'll devote solely to pampering himself. When it comes to hanging out, though, don't look for this brown-eyed cutie in fancy restaurants. To

Jordan still looks up to his older brother Jonathan.

Jordan's most memorable experience was playing at the Apollo Theater in New York.

Jordan thrills New Kids fans with his sweet
style and awesome vocal range.

find down-to-earth Jordan, check out the hamburger chains. He absolutely adores hamburgers and milk shakes. Jordan also loves good homemade lasagna.

If you're hooked on Jordan, you may also want to know that Jordan went through a "difficult" phase when he was younger. He used to spray paint graffiti on Boston subway walls. Luckily, his parents dealt with him fairly but firmly, and Jordan got his act straightened out.

Today, Jordan is known as the polite and well behaved New Kid. Girls who have been lucky enough to meet him have noted that he is the perfect gentleman. He opens doors for women and stands up whenever a lady enters the room.

Although all his brothers and sisters are musically talented, Jordan stood out from an early age. He used to be a soloist with the All Saints Church choir in Boston. And at the age of ten, he sang in the Boston Opera Company's production of Shakespeare's "Othello."

Jordan's parents encouraged his talent by enrolling him in summer music camps at Princeton University. A good pianist, Jordan admits that when he was younger, he even toyed with the idea of becoming a classical musician.

Jordan would have been great at anything he decided to pursue, but aren't you glad he chose rock 'n' roll instead? After all, how many classical musicians do you read about in teen mags?

Whether Jordan's sweet personality, good looks, and talent will someday lead him into an acting career, no one knows for certain. But one thing's for sure—this New Kid is bound to be around for a long time.

Although "J" likes touring, he hates leaving home.

JONATHAN KNIGHT

To many of his fans, tall, dark, and handsome Jonathan is the New Kids' Knight in shining armor. Although he's the oldest of the New Kids and sometimes plays big brother to the other guys, sweet and shy Jonathan is never one to steal the spotlight. In fact, he's the only New Kid who doesn't have a solo song on *Hangin' Tough*.

"I didn't feel ready for it," he told *Bop* magazine. "Maybe on the next one I will."

Jonathan often takes a back seat to his more visible and vocal brother, Jordan, who's also in New Kids. But anyone who thinks his role in the New Kids on the Block is any less important couldn't be more wrong. As talented as

continued on page 64

Jonathan looked awfully cute during a party at
The Palladium in New York City.

He may be quiet offstage, but Jonathan knows how to rock the socks off his fans.

he is quiet, Jonathan is a major force in the band.

As a child, Jonathan was a little less shy. He and younger brother Jordan used to sing in their church choir, impressing churchgoers with their beautiful harmonizing. Born Jonathan Rasleigh Knight in Worcester, Massachusetts, on November 29, 1968, Jonathan was encouraged by his mother to pursue whatever he was interested in when he

Jonathan thinks that drugs stink!

New Kids *(left to right)* Jordan Knight, Donnie Wahlberg, Danny Wood, Jonathan Knight, and Joe McIntyre are buddies as well as bandmates.

DANNY

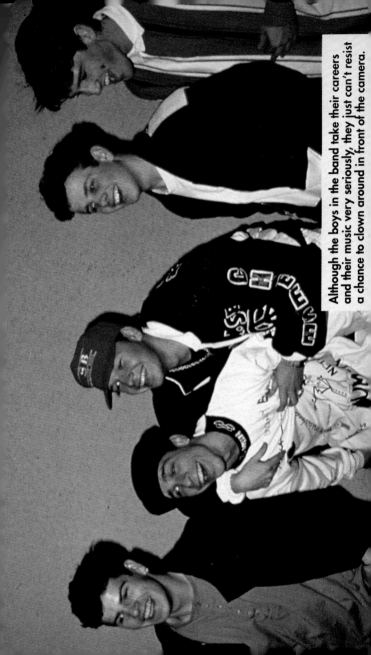

Although the boys in the band take their careers and their music very seriously, they just can't resist a chance to clown around in front of the camera.

In concert, the New Kids on the Block give their fans plenty to scream and shout about with their smooth dance moves and fun-loving spirit.

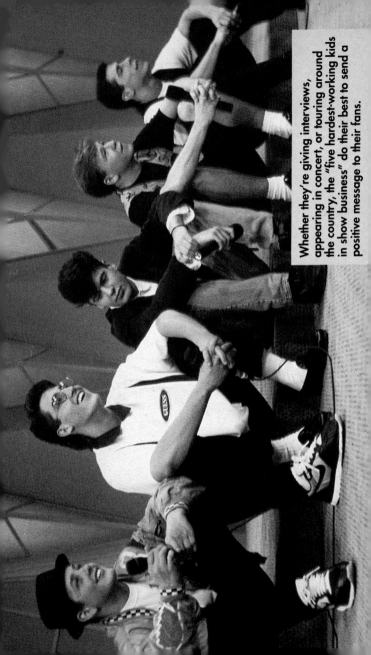

Whether they're giving interviews, appearing in concert, or touring around the country, the "five hardest-working kids in show business" do their best to send a positive message to their fans.

Each of the New Kids has his own unique image, his own style. Together, they've taken the music world by storm and captured the hearts of fans around the world.

NO BALL PLAYING

No one knows what the future holds for the fab five. But the New Kids on the Block plan on hangin' around—and hangin' tough—for a long time.

was growing up. When he told her that he wanted to become a musician, she didn't try to discourage him. For this, Jonathan will always be thankful.

"It's difficult enough growing up, but without the support of your parents, it's almost impossible," Jonathan told *Teen Beat* magazine. "I was lucky to get such encouragement from her."

Even at such a young age, Jonathan knew that music would play an important

Jon was happy to pose with his mom, Marlene Putnam.

Jon looks like he needs a dancing partner. Any volunteers?

Jonathan puckers up for his pooch, Nikko.

role in his life. And when his parents
suggested he spend his summers working
at his singing, he jumped at the chance.
While some of his school friends spent
their summers looking for things to do,
Jonathan attended the Royal School of
Church Music, which was held at various
college campuses across the country. And
when Jonathan was in high school, he
enjoyed singing and acting in musicals.

All that hard work and devotion
began paying off when Jonathan joined
the New Kids. Now, he's a star in the
music world. He also hopes that, when
things calm down with New Kids, he can

continued on page 70

67

Debbie Gibson popped in for a backstage chat with Jordan and Jon after a New Kids concert in New York.

The three "J"s jam for the fans.

get back into acting, as well. Don't worry, though—Jonathan is not leaving the band to become an actor. Music is his first love, and he would never let his fans down by quitting the group.

Jonathan says he enjoys almost all the aspects of being a celebrity, except one. Although he appreciates the

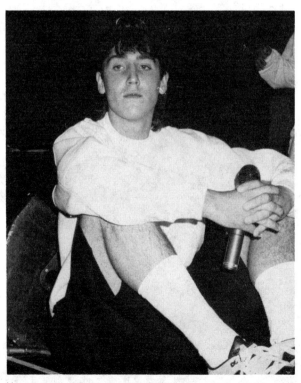

Wonder who Jonathan is thinking about?

Could this be sweet Jonathan's dream house?

affection of his fans, it bothers him that he can't do normal things without fans noticing.

"Like when we come back from a show, there's always a lot of kids running around the hotel," he told *Teen Beat* magazine. "After a show, we just want to take a shower and go to bed. So we'll take showers and run out into the hallway in a bathrobe, and there'll be all these girls standing there and then they all start screaming."

Fortunately for his fans, this bashful boy is learning to deal with all the attention.

JOE McINTYRE

Baby-faced Joey McIntyre is cute and lovable. Born in Needham, Massachusetts, on December 31, 1972, he's the youngest member of New Kids on the Block. But, make no mistake about it, Joe's not a kid anymore.

"I think people think I'm a lot younger than I actually am," he told *The Associated Press.* "It's because I was so much shorter than all the other guys for a while. I'm finally catching up."

With his sandy blond hair and sparkling blue eyes, Joe certainly has the looks of a star. He may be shy about his boyish good looks, but ask anyone who has seen him up-close and personal, and they'll tell you that Joe is one major cutie.

As the youngest New Kid, Joe also takes a lot of playful teasing from his bandmates, but he shrugs off the friendly

Joe settles in for a nice long talk. Could this doll have *your* number?

Joey Joe wants to know how you feel about
the New Kids on the Block.

Joe used to act in community theater in Boston.

ribbing with ease. They wouldn't tease
him unless they liked him, right? Besides,
Joe is confident of his musical ability.

Many of you are probably
wondering just where Joe gets all his
talent. While he was no doubt born with
a good deal of it, his mom and dad did

**Joe takes a break after a long day of making
music.**

The New Kids' All-American boy shows off his spirit on stage.

a great deal to foster his interest in performing. Joe's parents aren't famous stars. His father, Thomas, is a vice-president of the Bricklayers International Union, and his mother, Kay, is a secretary. But, instead of spending their evenings watching television when Joe was growing up, they chose to take part in community theater.

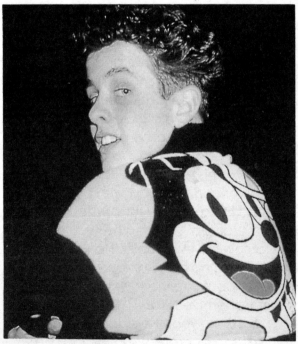

Joe isn't that picky about his clothes. He'll wear anything that fits well.

Joe and his nine brothers and sisters caught the acting bug from watching their parents perform. At just six years of age, adorable Joey began costarring in Boston productions of classics like "Oliver Twist" and "The Music Man." Around Boston, he was known as a talented young actor who happened to sing.

Then, the New Kids happened, and people began paying more attention to Joe's musical talents. His smooth, sultry singing style reminds many older people of singers they grew up listening to. Joe, himself, likes Frank Sinatra, a man old enough to be his grandfather!

Joe is very serious about being a musician, but he is also serious about his education. While some other kids his age complain about having to go to school, Joe enjoys his studies. He takes his schoolwork on the road with him and studies with a private tutor who travels with the group. Joe says he would like to go to college eventually. He wouldn't mind trying his hand at journalism. He says his ideal interview would be with actor Robert De Niro.

And, like Jonathan, Joe would like to take a stab at professional acting. He's already got an edge in that department.

Joe's sultry voice and baby-blue eyes remind many parents of Joe's idol, Frank Sinatra.

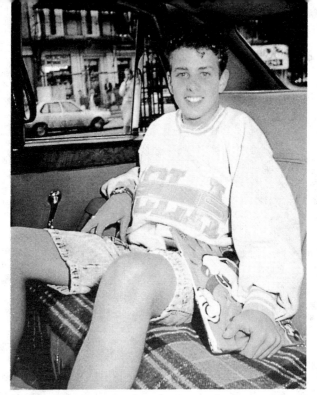

Even when he's on the road, Joe finds time for his schoolwork.

In addition to his looks and talent, he gets tips on performing from his sister Judy, who's an actress in New York.

For now, however, Joe's number-one priority is being in New Kids on the Block. So, he's going to continue to thrill fans with his sweet voice and darling blue eyes. And he's going to keep on signing

Looks like Joe was in a hurry as he arrived in
Los Angeles for the American Music Awards.

autographs, chillin', and munching on spicy Mexican food.

"It's a real good time, even if it only lasts a month or more or a year or more or a decade or more, whatever," Joe told Don McLeese of the *Chicago Sun-Times*. "It doesn't matter. I'm still young. I've got my whole life ahead of me."

"I am just really happy to be a part of all this," he told *Tiger Beat* magazine. "I can't think of anything more exciting to happen to a kid."

When he's not working, Joe enjoys playing basketball, bowling, and just chillin'.

THE NEW KIDS ROCK THE BLOCK

Donnie is walking around backstage trying to work off some of his pent-up energy. He can hear the fans' high-pitched squeals, begging the New Kids on the Block to come on stage. It's difficult to determine who's more anxious—the sell-out crowd that is waiting for the band, or Donnie, who wants to get out there and sing.

"Performing live is a real rush for us," Donnie says. "You can't imagine what it's like to feel that connection with the kids. It's like they know we're there for the same reason they are—to have a good time."

Meanwhile, a voice comes over the amplifiers. "Please welcome the five

continued on page 86

83

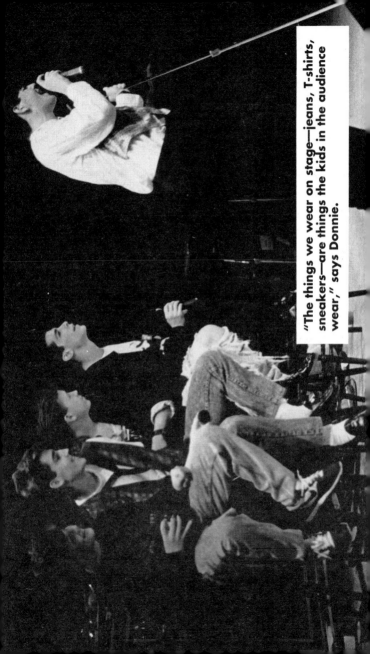

"The things we wear on stage—jeans, T-shirts, sneakers—are things the kids in the audience wear," says Donnie.

Donnie, Danny, and Jordan call themselves the Crickets when they work on new tunes for the band.

hardest-working kids in show business!"

The lights go down, and the audience starts to scream again. Girls jump up and down, trying to get a glimpse of their idols. When the New Kids on the Block hit the stage, the roar of thunderous applause fills the stadium.

This is the showplace that veteran rockers like David Bowie and Rod Stewart failed to sell out. The New Kids on the Block have played to sell-out crowds here not once but four times.

To their fans, the New Kids are Donnie, Danny, Jon, Joe, and Jordan. Last names aren't necessary, because everyone here knows who the boys are. You can't be a true fan if you don't.

It also helps to know their songs by heart, because for much of the show, the fans join in. Their voices echo in the background as the New Kids belt out hits like "Hangin' Tough," "You Got It (The Right Stuff)," and "Cover Girl." The New Kids appreciate the response. They show their affection, in turn, by talking to their fans between songs.

Although every fan dreams of being front-row center at the New Kids' concert, only a few lucky concertgoers get this honor. Fortunately, the New Kids go out

It's no wonder Donnie and Jordan work well together. They were pals before they joined the New Kids.

of their way to make everyone, especially those fans sitting way up in the balcony, feel they are just a few feet away.

Unlike some stars, who are more interested in making money than pleasing their fans, the New Kids go all

Joe tries to add a personal touch to his performance whenever he's on stage.

out to make eye contact with the kids who've come to see them perform. They constantly grin and run across the stage waving at their fans. It's a wonder that they don't run into each other.

At one point between songs, the

continued on page 92

"We've got a lot of energy and excitement," says Jordan. **"Kids can definitely relate to it."**

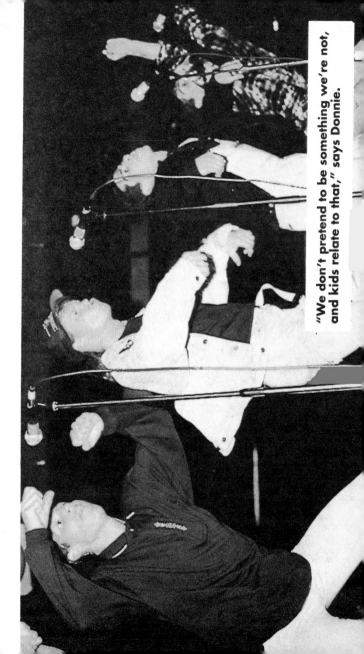

"We don't pretend to be something we're not, and kids relate to that," says Donnie.

The boys pump it up and take it to the bridge.

The boys are so full of energy on stage, it's no surprise they play to sell-out crowds.

youngest New Kid, Joe, looks into the sea of faces and asks, "Can we take it to the bridge?" The crowd answers back, "Take it to the bridge!" His bandmates chime in, "Pump it up, homeboys, just like that," and the boys begin a hip new dance.

"Budding" artist Jordan arrives in style at the American Music Awards.

Jonathan, Joe, Donnie, and Jordan get into
some great harmonizing to the delight of
screaming fans.

The New Kids are great in concert. They play songs from their albums, but they also add little variations that make each tune sound a bit different. Jordan adds just a little more sweetness to his voice as he sings the ballad "Didn't I (Blow Your Mind)." And the boys' rendition of "Stop It Girl," from their self-titled debut album, is both sad and forceful.

"We love you," Jordan says at the end of the evening. He blows kisses and accepts flowers from some of the girls who manage to get up close to the stage. Before bodyguards haul the girls off, one of them gets a quick kiss from Jordan. And then, the stage lights go down and the boys are gone. They're off to another city to make more dreams come true.

ON THE ROAD WITH THE NEW KIDS

Going on the road can be fun, or it can be a chore, depending on how you look at it. If the idea of performing in a different city every night sounds like torture to you, then you probably couldn't keep up with the New Kids on the Block. These boys live for touring.

"There's nothing like seeing your fans enjoy your show to give you a big thrill," Donnie says. "We live for it. That's what rock is all about."

Before every tour, the New Kids have to take a look at what cities they'll be performing in. If the tour is limited to the East Coast or the West Coast, it's pretty easy for them to pack their clothes. But on most tours, the boys end up playing in a variety of places across the country. And

The New Kids on the Block show off their
awards backstage at the 17th Annual American
Music Awards.

On stage as well as behind the scenes, the boys in the band are like brothers.

that often means being prepared for balmy breezes as well as icy winds.

When the boys first started touring, they ended up packing everything but the kitchen sink. By now, however, they've learned to pack wisely and not load up their luggage with too much junk. Does Donnie really need all the multicolored Jams? And can Jon live without bringing all his favorite books?

One good thing about having to pack lightly is that it gives the boys an excuse to visit local shopping malls while they're on tour. Sightseeing is tough when you're touring on a tight schedule, but on their occasional days off from work, the boys like to shop for clothes and buy presents for their friends and family back home in Boston.

"Part of the great joy of success is being able to share it with your loved ones," Donnie notes. "We won't always be popular, so we have to take advantage of our situation now."

It's hard to believe the New Kids could ever NOT be popular. Everywhere you turn you see their gorgeous faces or hear their smooth voices. You can catch them on the radio, in magazines, on posters, on television, and even on their own 900 telephone line. And if you're lucky, you can see them live on stage.

Although it sounds glamorous to travel across the country and around the world on tour, being on the road can also be tough sometimes. That's especially true for the New Kids, because they all come from close-knit families. Being away from your parents and siblings can be hard, especially when you're young. Luckily, the boys are like brothers, so their homesickness isn't as bad as it could be if they were traveling alone.

continued on page 102

The guys were ready to roll in the United Cerebral Palsy Bike-a-Thon in New York City. The New Kids are the official teen spokesmen for UCP.

The New Kids were looking dapper for the taping of the Grammy Living Legends tribute in Hollywood.

"We take care of each other," Donnie says. "It's not like we'll stop each other from eating junk food, like our moms would. That's one of the good things about being on the road. But we'll try to make sure everyone's OK, you know what I mean?"

We sure do, Donnie.

The guys goof off in front of the camera at the Kids Choice Awards in Los Angeles.

MAKING RECORDS
AND VIDEOS

The boys in New Kids on the Block
are still in the early stages of their careers.
But they're working hard to make a
name for themselves as serious musicians.
To these kids, that means presenting an
honest, positive, and upbeat image of
themselves in both their music and their
videos.

"When we make our records, we try
to be true to our music and the spirit of
the band," says Donnie. "But that doesn't
mean we want to do the same thing
each time. That would be boring, and I
don't think that's what the fans want. And
that's certainly not what we want."

Anyone who has heard the Kids' first
three albums knows that the group is
willing to try new things. On their latest
album, *Step by Step*, they once again

show their ability to experiment and grow. While it has the same lively spirit that made *Hangin' Tough* such an international hit, the New Kids' latest also offers fans something new.

"We've always liked changing," Donnie says. "We don't think it's worth rehashing previous hits, no matter how good they were."

They feel the same way about videos. While all their videos so far have been pretty much "live" action, the New Kids are interested in shooting a couple of pieces based on a concept or story. And with the Kids getting older, it's likely

The New Kids donated the profits from "This One's for the Children" to United Cerebral Palsy.

The New Kids practice their dance moves over and over to make sure every step looks just right.

that the storylines will eventually include romance.

No matter what kinds of videos they do in the future, though, there's one thing that will remain the same—the boys will want to have as much input as possible. That means that if the director asks them to do something they don't feel good about or that isn't true to the spirit of the band, they'll ask him if they can do something else. Their ideas are almost always adhered to.

"We have a lot more input than people think," Donnie says. "Just 'cause we're young doesn't mean we can't think for ourselves."

The guys take pride in the group's positive image.

NEW KIDS
IN A NUTSHELL

"I think the key to any success is being happy with who you are and who you work with," says Donnie.

DANNY WOOD

Full name: Daniel William Wood, Jr.
Nicknames: Puff McLoud, Woody the Woodpecker
Birth date: May 14, 1969
Birthplace: Boston, Massachusetts
Eye color: Chestnut brown
Hair color: Black
Height: 5'8"
Weight: 145 lbs.
Parents: Daniel, Sr., and Elizabeth
Siblings: Bethany, Pam, Brett, Rachel, Melissa
Favorite holiday: Christmas
Favorite book: *The Autobiography of Malcolm X*
What he does in his spare time: On Thursday night, when he's just relaxing, he watches *The Cosby Show*. When he's feeling more active, he loves to play a good game of basketball.
First record he paid for: David Bowie's early 1980's dance hit, "Let's Dance"
Favorite type of girl: Danny likes nice girls who have a good sense of humor. It also helps if they're cute.
Favorite food: Anything that doesn't move. In particular, he enjoys Chinese and Italian food.

Danny and his "dancing" flower chill to some way cool tunes.

DONNIE WAHLBERG

Full name: Donald E. Wahlberg, Jr.
Nicknames: Dennis Cheese, and, of
 course, Donnie
Birth date: August 17, 1969
Birthplace: Dorchester, Massachusetts
Height: 5'10"
Weight: 155 lbs.
Eye color: Hazel
Hair color: Blondish brown
Parents: Donald, Sr., and Alma
Siblings: Michelle, Debbie, Paul, Arthur,
 Jimbo, Tracey, Bob, and Mark
Shirt size: Large
Shoe size: 8
Favorite food: His father's down-home
 cooking
Favorite TV show: *Sesame Street* (No
 kidding!)
Favorite type of girl: A fun, independent-
 minded girl who has got a lot of spirit
Bad habit: He eats way too much junk
 food.
Words of advice: "Peace out." "Just say no
 to drugs!"

What's this tough guy's message? "Peace out!"

JORDAN KNIGHT

Full name: Jordan Nathaniel Marcel Knight

Nickname: "J"

Birth date: May 17, 1971

Birthplace: Worcester, Massachusetts

Height: 5'10"

Weight: 155 lbs.

Eye color: Brown

Hair color: Dark brown

Parents: Marlene Putnam and Allan Knight

Siblings: Allison, Sharon, David, Chris, and fellow New Kid Jon

Favorite movies: *Robocop* and *The Untouchables*

Pets: A couple of adorable Siamese cats named Buster and Misty

Favorite song: "You Make Me Feel Brand New" by the Stylistics

First job: Camp counselor

Did you know...that Jordan was chased out of a store by a man with a gun? Jordan wasn't doing anything wrong. The man mistakenly thought Jordan was writing graffiti on the walls of his store.

This jazzy young gentleman opens doors for
ladies.

JON KNIGHT

Full name: Jonathan Rasleigh Knight
Nickname: "GQ"
Birth date: November 29, 1968
Birthplace: Worcester, Massachusetts
Height: 5'11"
Weight: 155 lbs.
Eye color: Hazel
Hair color: Brown
Parents: Marlene Putnam and Allan Knight
Siblings: Allison, Sharon, David, Chris, and, of course, Jordan
Favorite foods: Milk shakes, hamburgers, French fries, chocolate bars, and cupcakes
Favorite sports: He enjoys individual sports, such as skiing and swimming.
Favorite colors: He likes the dramatic effect of combining black and white.
Best childhood memory: Spending summers with his grandparents in their Canadian cottage
He hates: Heavy metal music. He doesn't think many of the musicians are very talented at what they do.
Favorite type of girl: Jon likes a girl that he can talk to. Pretty girls are fine, but intelligence really captivates him.

Jon says he wants the New Kid's music to change and grow with the times.

JOE McINTYRE

Full name: Joseph Mulrey McIntyre
Nicknames: Joe Bird (because of his
   amazing vocal pitch), Joey Joe
Birth date: December 31, 1972
Birthplace: Needham, Massachusetts
Height: 5'6"
Weight: 120 lbs.
Eye color: Blue
Hair color: Blondish brown
Parents: Thomas and Kay
Siblings: Judith, Alice, Susan, Patricia,
   Carol, Jean, Kate, and Tom
Shirt size: Small
Shoe size: 8 1/2
Favorite drink: Anything nonalcoholic,
   especially Classic Coke
Favorite food: Spicy. He adores Mexican
   cuisine.
Favorite colors: Red and blue
Movies that make him laugh: *Big* and
   Beverly Hills Cop
Heroes in the entertainment world: Actors
   Bill Cosby and Robert De Niro
Musical instrument: Guitar
Did you know...that Joe travels with a
   good-luck teddy bear when he's on
   tour?

Joe is trying to wean himself of his Classic Coke habit.

FUN FACTS

Be the first on the block to know these
facts about the New Kids:

Jon thinks that his best quality is that he is
good-natured.

The Japanese girls apparently like cute
Danny the best. Even though they can't
speak English very well, they manage to
get their messages across in love notes.

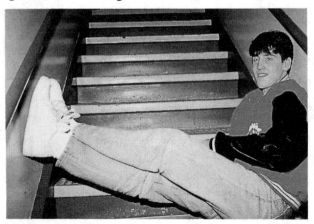

**Laid-back Jon loves spending the day watching
movies.**

Of all the New Kids, Jon has the largest
feet. He wears size $10^1/_2$ shoes.

Joe's favorite musical groups are the Temptations and Huey Lewis and the News.

Do you know that April 24, 1989, was proclaimed "New Kids on the Block Day" in Massachusetts?

"I love to hang out and just do nothing," says "J".

Even though he thinks touring is glamorous, Jordan hates leaving home.

Do you remember the New Kids' first single? It was "Be My Girl."

Merry, Merry Christmas was the highest-charting Christmas album since John Denver's *Rocky Mountain High* in 1975.

Donnie is a romantic at heart. His idea of a perfect date is a quiet dinner for two, followed by a slow walk around his favorite spots in Boston.

Danny says his pants ripped once or twice on stage.

Danny's favorite musician is the New Kids' record producer, Maurice Starr. Starr is famous for bringing the New Kids together and for putting together another fab group, New Edition.

Danny's ideal car is not a BMW or a Porsche. He prefers the rugged Cherokee Jeep.

One of Danny's favorite songs is "Some Things Never Change" by the Stylistics.

When he has time, Joe enjoys watching the comedy series *Cheers.*

Even though he's traveled around the world, one of Joe's favorite spots is Disney World, right here in the U.S. of A.

Donnie says that, for him, the ideal costar in a movie would be Cher.

Of the five musicians in the New Kids on the Block, Donnie has the most checkered past. As a child, he was, by his own account, a borderline juvenile delinquent who occasionally shoplifted. He soon realized what he was doing was wrong. Today, he encourages kids to think before doing anything so stupid.

Friends say Donnie does a great Michael Jackson impersonation.

VIDEOGRAPHY

SINGLES
"Please Don't Go Girl"
"You Got It (The Right Stuff)"
"I'll Be Loving You (Forever)"
"Hangin' Tough"
"Cover Girl"
"This One's for the Children"

COMPILATIONS
Hangin' Tough
"Please Don't Go Girl"
"You Got It (The Right Stuff)"
"I'll Be Loving You (Forever)"
"Hangin' Tough"

Hangin' Tough Live
"My Favorite Girl"
"What'cha Gonna Do (About It)"
"Please Don't Go Girl"
"Cover Girl"
"You Got It (The Right Stuff)"
"I'll Be Loving You (Forever)"
"Hangin' Tough"

The New Kids insist that their current success is just the beginning.

DISCOGRAPHY

Hangin' Tough

New Kids on the Block

Merry, Merry Christmas

Step By Step

The New Kids' *Hangin' Tough* **album went quintuple platinum in Japan.**

NEW KIDS QUIZ

How much do you know about the New Kids on the Block? Some of the answers can be found scattered throughout the book (as well as on page 128). Give it a go. Good luck.

1) Who wears a gold earring that is shaped like a G-clef?

2) What's the weirdest question the New Kids have been asked?

3) Which New Kid has been romantically linked with teenage-singer Tiffany?

4) Who is the only New Kid who still has to do homework?

5) Which one of the guys is a Mexican-food fanatic?

6) What was Jon's favorite childhood toy?

7) What job did Danny hold while he was waiting for *Hangin' Tough* to take off?

8) What instrument does Jordan play?

9) The New Kids on the Block became the first teen group to do what?

10) How long did it take for *Hangin' Tough* to reach No. 1?

There's no denying that the New Kids on the Block have got the right stuff!

Answers from quiz on page 126:

1) Danny.
2) "Would you eat a live bowl of crickets for $40,000?" The answer, by the way, is a resounding "NO!"
3) All of them have been rumored to be romantically interested in Tiffany.
4) Joe.
5) Joe.
6) Hot Wheels cars.
7) He was a courier who delivered airline tickets.
8) Keyboards.
9) They hit No. 1 on the Hot 100 and the Top Pop Album charts simultaneously.
10) Fifty-five weeks. It's a good thing the boys hung tough.

To tell the New Kids how much they mean to you, write to:

New Kids on the Block
P.O. Box 7001
Quincy, MA 02269